Mairi's Mermaid

Crabtree Publishing Company
www.crabtreebooks.com

PMB 16A, 350 Fifth Avenue,
Suite 3308,
New York, NY 10118

616 Welland Avenue,
St. Catharines, Ontario
Canada, L2M 5V6

Morpurgo, Michael.
  Mairi's mermaid / written by Michael Morpurgo;
illustrated by Lucy Richards.
    p. cm. -- (Blue bananas)
  Summary: Mairi has trouble learning to swim until she meets a tiny mermaid
who needs her help.
  ISBN-13: 978-0-7787-0851-3 (rlb)
  ISBN-10: 0-7787-0851-9 (rlb)
  ISBN-13: 978-0-7787-0897-1 (pbk)
  ISBN-10: 0-7787-0897-7 (pbk)
  [1. Swimming--Fiction. 2. Mermaids--Fiction.] I. Richards, Lucy, ill. II.
Title. III. Series.
  PZ7.M82712Mai 2006
  [E]--dc22

2005035765

LC

Published by Crabtree Publishing in 2006
First published in 2001 by Egmont Books Ltd.
Text copyright © Michael Morpurgo 1994
Illustrations © Lucy Richards 2001
The Author and Illustrator have asserted their moral rights.
Paperback ISBN 0-7787-0897-7
Reinforced Hardcover Binding ISBN 0-7787-0851-9

1 2 3 4 5 6 7 8 9 0 Printed in Italy 5 4 3 2 1 0 9 8 7 6

Mairi's Mermaid

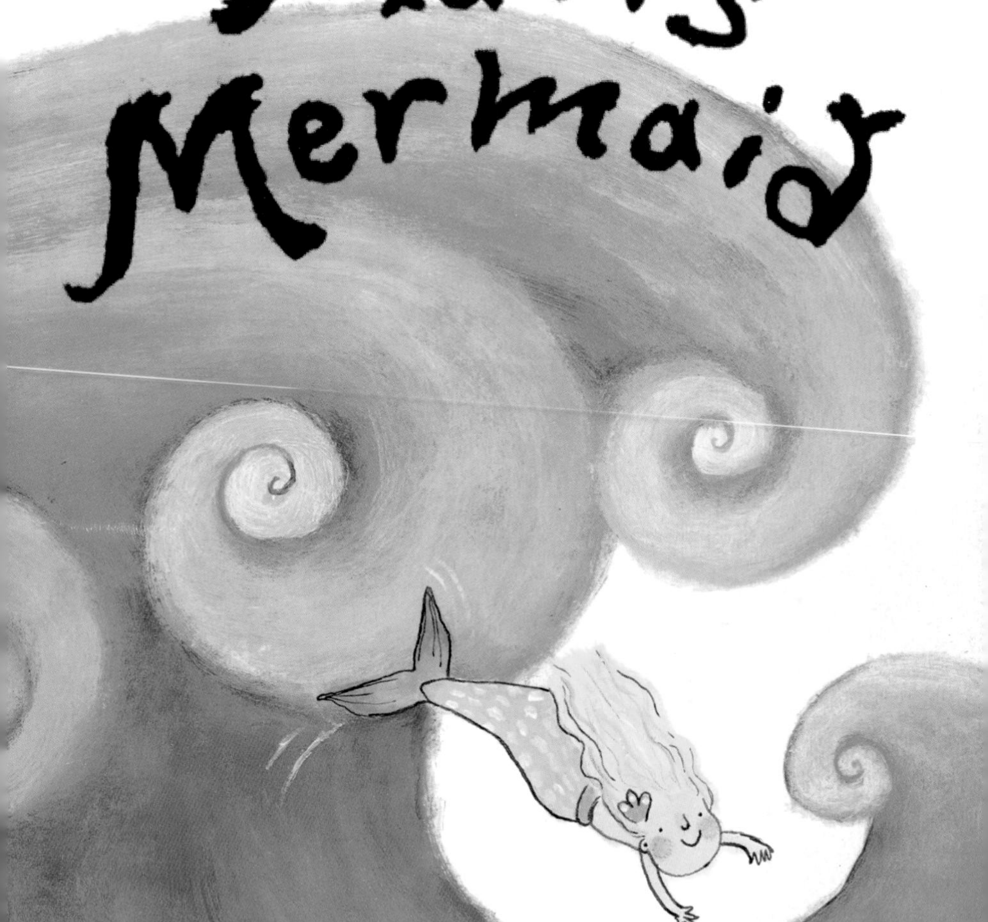

Michael Morpurgo
Illustrated by Lucy Richards

Blue Bananas

For Alan
M.M.

For Grandad Eric
and all my family
L.R.

Mairi still could not swim. She wished she could, but she just couldn't.

All throughout her vacation she'd been trying, but every time she took her feet off the bottom she sank like a stone.

Her brother Robbie swam like a fish.

"It's easy," he told her. "You believe in

mermaids don't you? Well, just pretend

you're a mermaid, like this."

He swims like a fish!

He laughed and plunged headfirst into another towering green wave. Sometimes Robbie was a real show-off.

Mairi's mother and father tried to help.

"It'll come," they said. "You'll do it."

But it didn't come and she didn't do it.

Mairi wanted to be miserable all

on her own.

She went to look for crabs in the rock pools and tried to forget all about swimming.

Soon she had collected five little crabs in her bucket. They'd be her pets for the day. Later she'd let them go and watch them swim away into the sea.

The water in the rock pool was warm from the sun. A shoal of silver fish darted around her legs. She could see a starfish and some sea anemones. "Swimming looks so easy for them," she thought.

That's a funny looking fish!

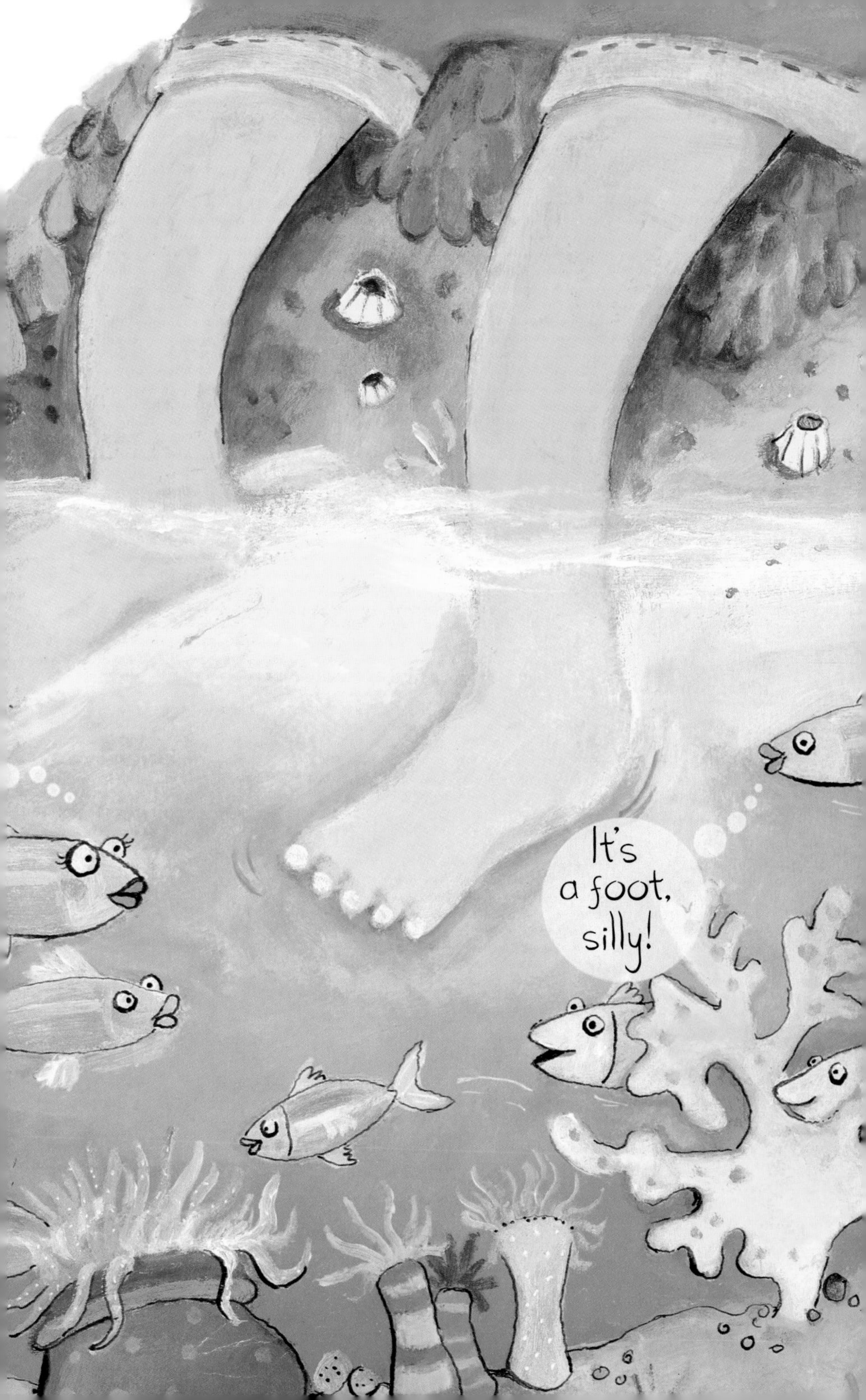
It's a foot, silly!

Suddenly something pinched her toe. She thought it might be a crab and jumped up. It was nothing. Maybe she had imagined it. But just to be sure, she decided not to dangle her feet again.

And then she heard a piping voice. It
seemed at first to come from far away.
She listened again. It came from deep
down in the rock pool.

Mairi brushed aside the seaweed and
there, glaring up at her, was a huge
brown crab. In his great grasping claw
was a fish, no bigger than her finger.

But then she saw it wasn't an ordinary
fish. It was a fish with arms and hands,
a fish with a head like her own and a
mouth that spoke. It was a little
mermaid.

Mairi was not at all afraid of crabs,
however big they were. She picked the
crab out of the water and shook him
and shook him.

The little mermaid dropped into the pool
and disappeared.

For a moment there was no sign of her.
Then a small head bobbed up. "Thank
you, oh, thank you," the mermaid said.

Mairi never knew mermaids could be
this small. She wasn't sure mermaids
were even real.

"Help me, please," said the mermaid.

"I went off on my own and I got stuck in this pool. Then that great big horrible crab caught me. He was going to eat me up!"

Of course I'm real!

Mairi would *so* like to have kept her as a pet for the day, but she knew what she had to do.

Mairi carried the little mermaid carefully
over the rocks and down to the sea.
Then she opened her hand, and let
the mermaid go. But the mermaid
wouldn't go.

I must
get home.

Little Mermaid, your mother is worried.

"No, no!" cried the little mermaid clutching Mairi's thumb. "Not here. The waves will smash me against the rocks. Take me out to that rock over there. Please! That's where we all live, in a big cave under that rock."

"But I can't swim," said Mairi.

21

"I'll tell you what," Mairi said. "I'll take you as far as I can walk, but I can't go out of my depth."

She stepped into the sea and waded out until the seawater came as high as her knees . . .

as high as her waist . . .

as high as her neck . . .

Suddenly a great wave came rolling in and lifted her right off her feet and when she came down there was no sandy bottom under her feet, no bottom at all.

Mairi kicked and
splashed and the
seawater went right
into her mouth.

Take a deep breath!

25

"It's all right," said the little mermaid.

"You're swimming!"

And when Mairi kicked again, she did not sink. She was swimming! She was!

I'm not sinking!

26

She lifted her chin and paddled through
the sea, keeping her mouth tightly closed.
Together, Mairi and the little mermaid
swam to the rock.

They were almost there when Mairi felt
an arm around her waist, then another
and another. The sea around her was
suddenly full of mermaids and mermen.
The little mermaid was clinging
to her mother's hair.

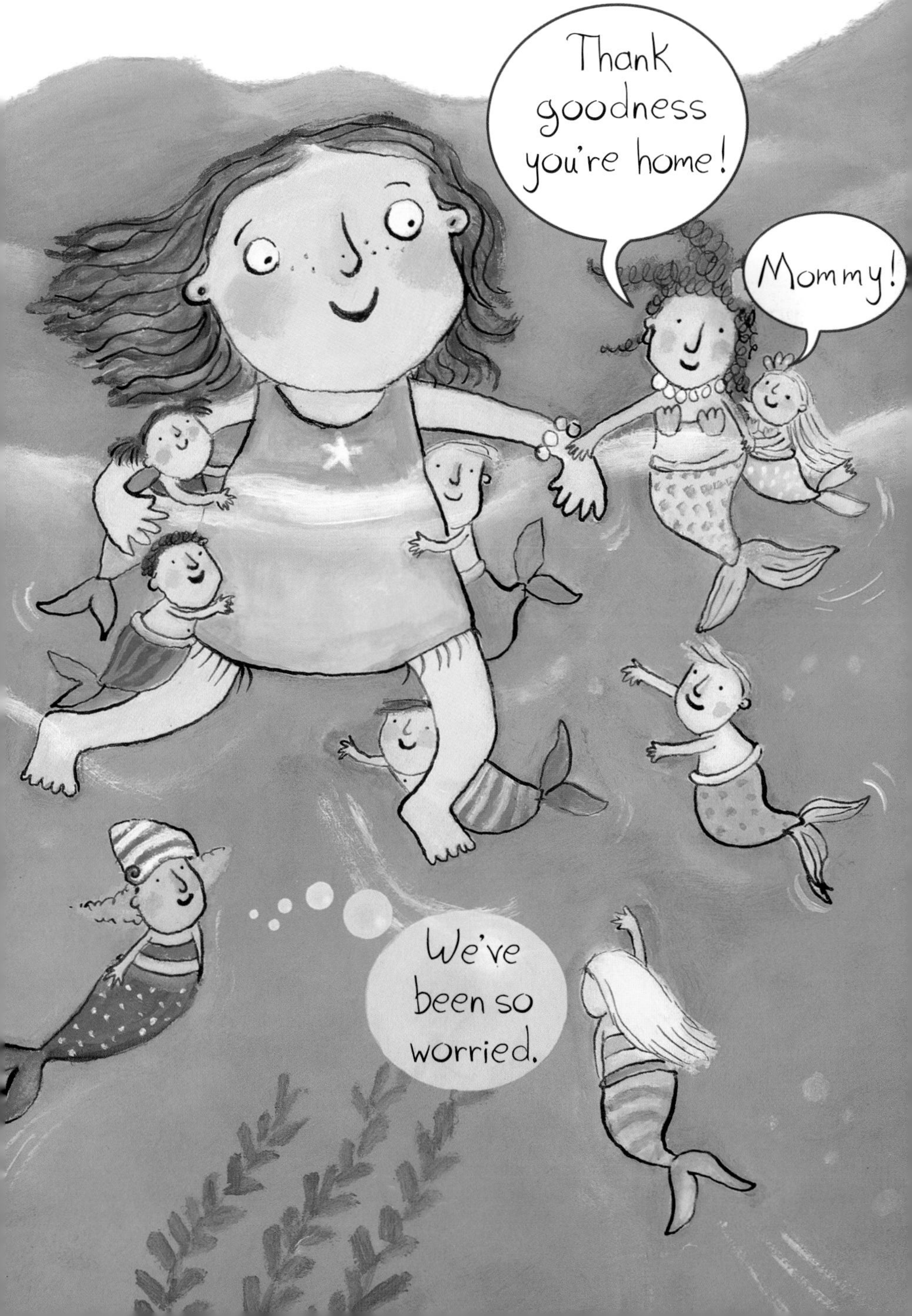
Thank goodness you're home!
Mommy!
We've been so worried.

Then Mairi felt the rock beneath her feet
and she could stand.

The little mermaid was telling everyone
her story. "Look what the
crab did to my tail,"
she said.

"Maybe it'll teach you not to go off like that," said her mother. "I've told you and told you. If it hadn't have been for this girl . . ." She smiled at Mairi. "How can we ever thank you?" she asked.

Mairi shook the crab!

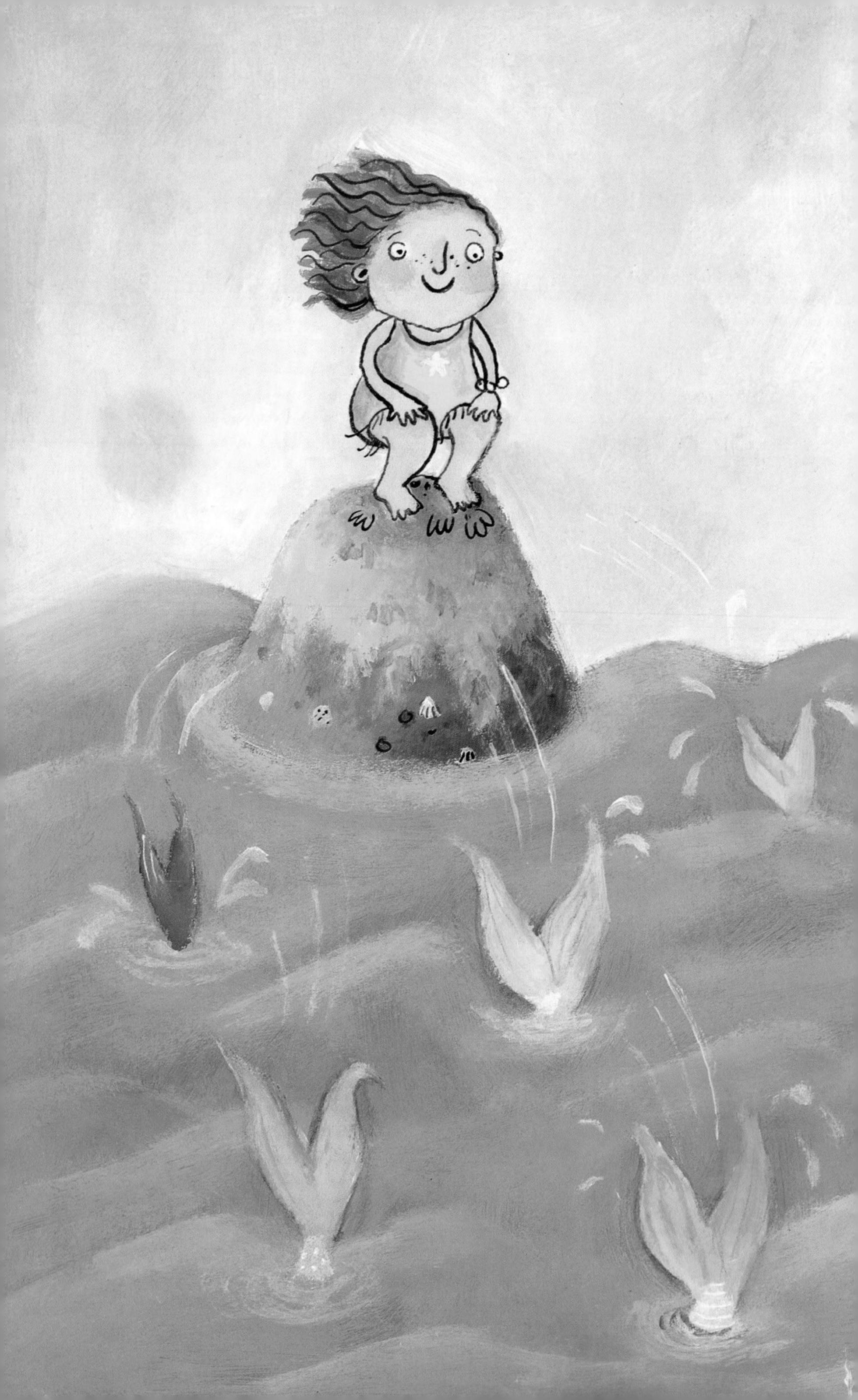

And Mairi had a sudden idea.

"You couldn't teach me how to swim, could you?" she asked. "I mean, like you do, like mermaids do."

First they taught her how to lie on the water and float. Mairi could feel the water holding her up!

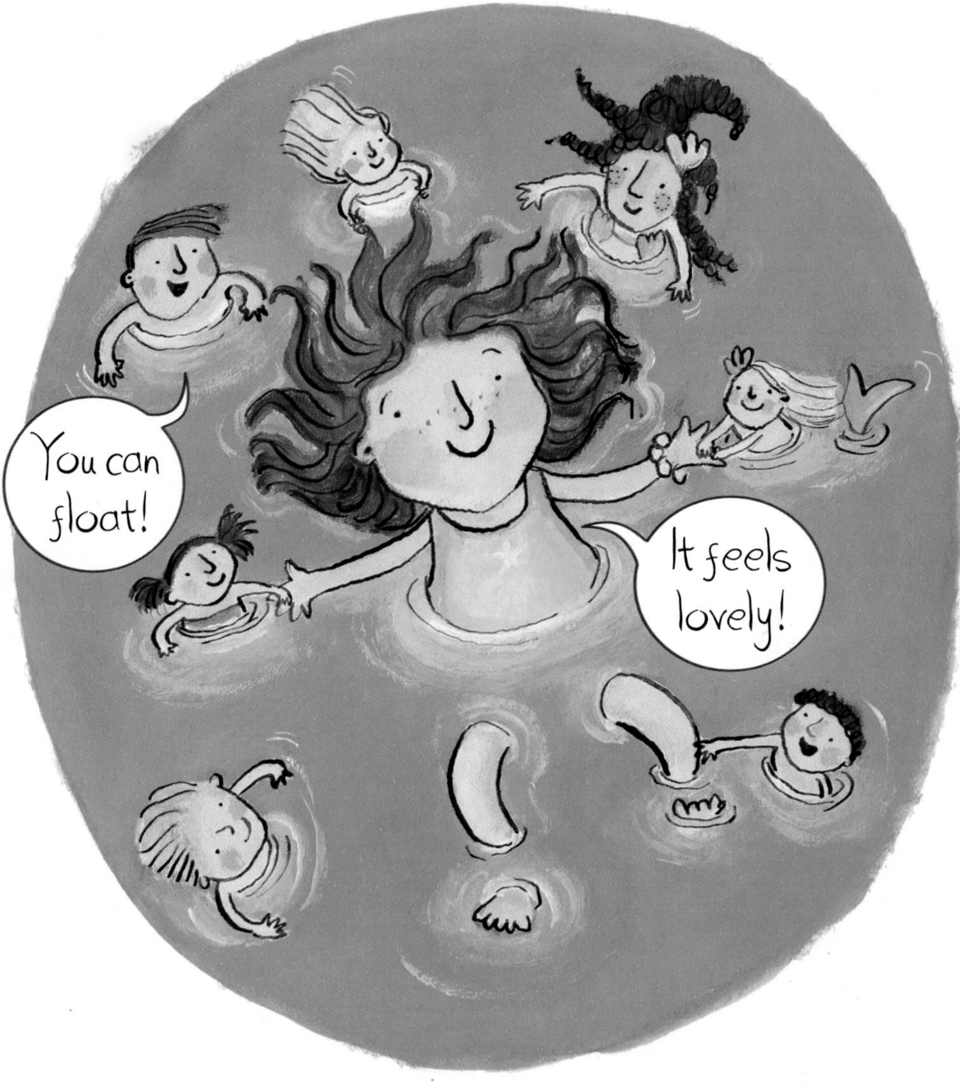
You can float!
It feels lovely!

Doggy
paddle was
next . . .

then

breaststroke . . .

then crawl . . .

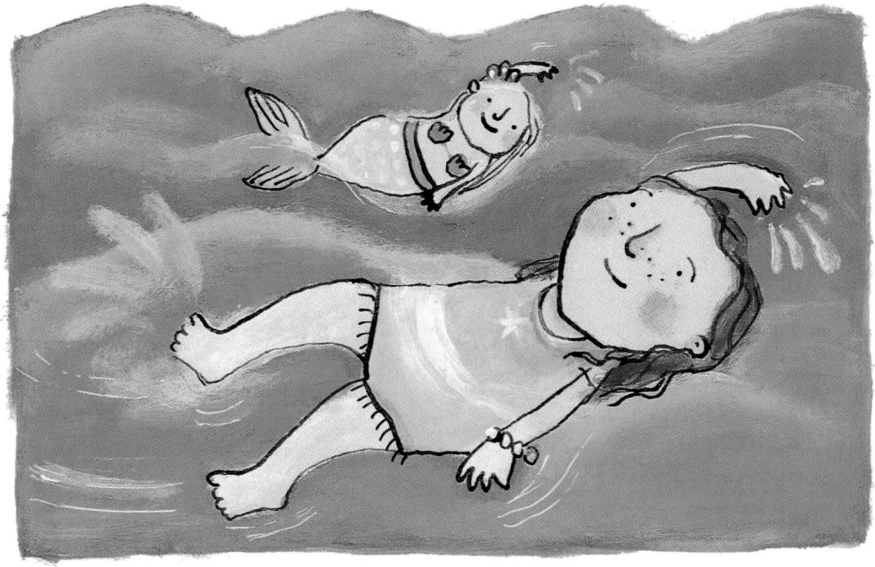

backstroke . . .

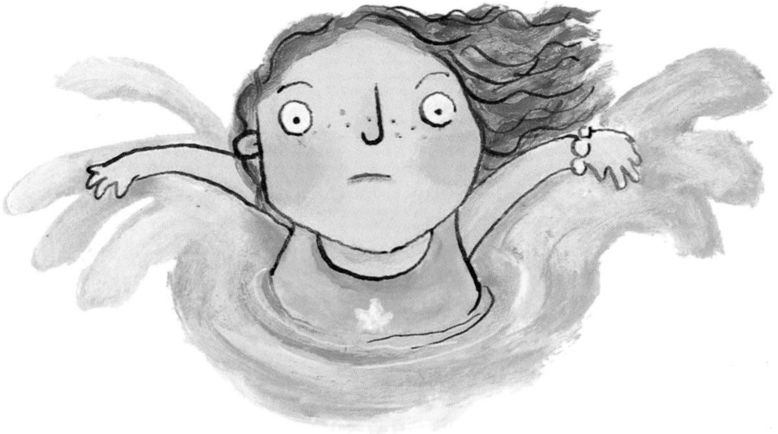

butterfly . . .

They even taught her to swim underwater!

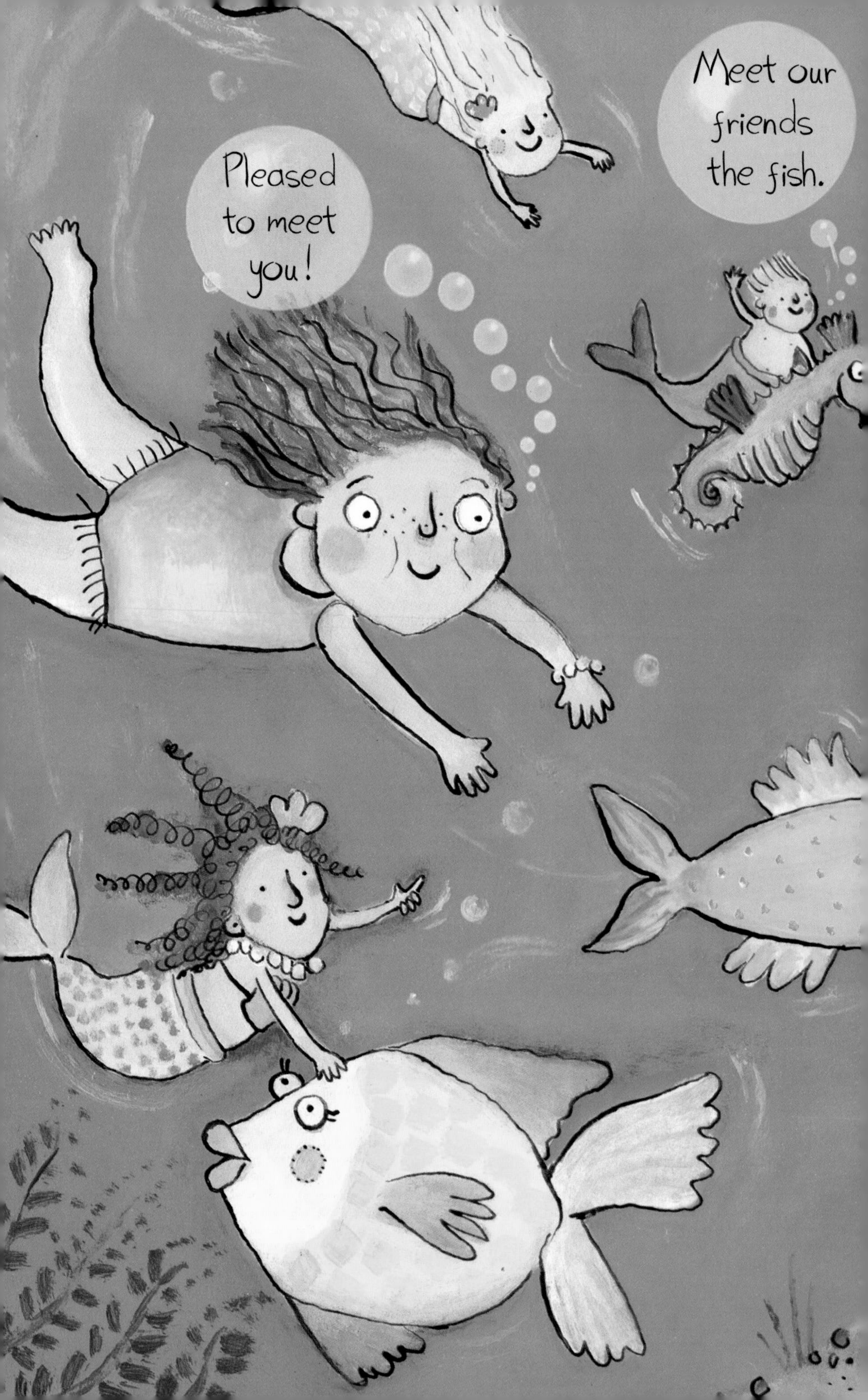
Pleased to meet you!
Meet our friends the fish.

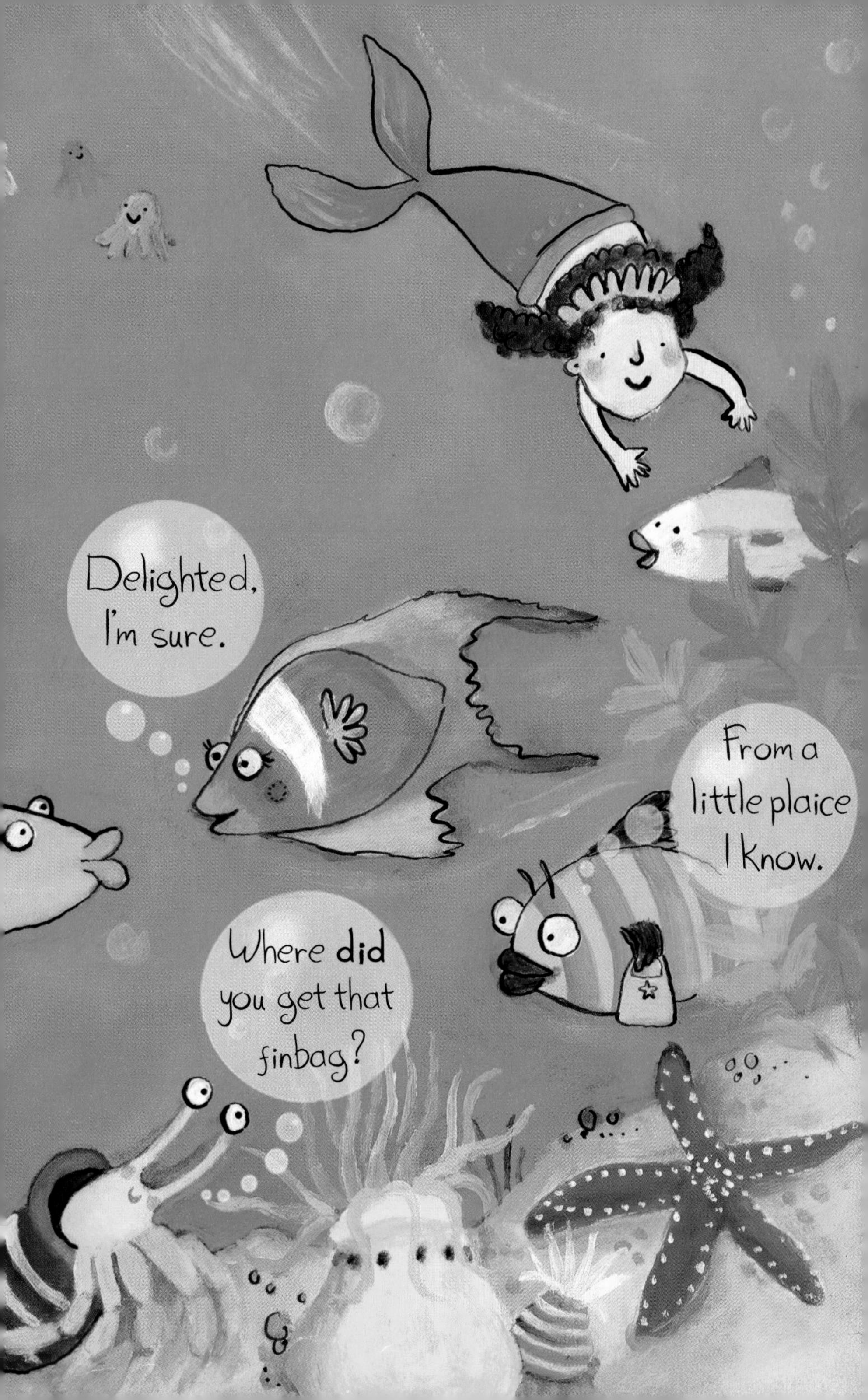
Delighted, I'm sure.
From a little plaice I know.
Where **did** you get that finbag?

Mairi wasn't afraid of the sea anymore.

She loved it!

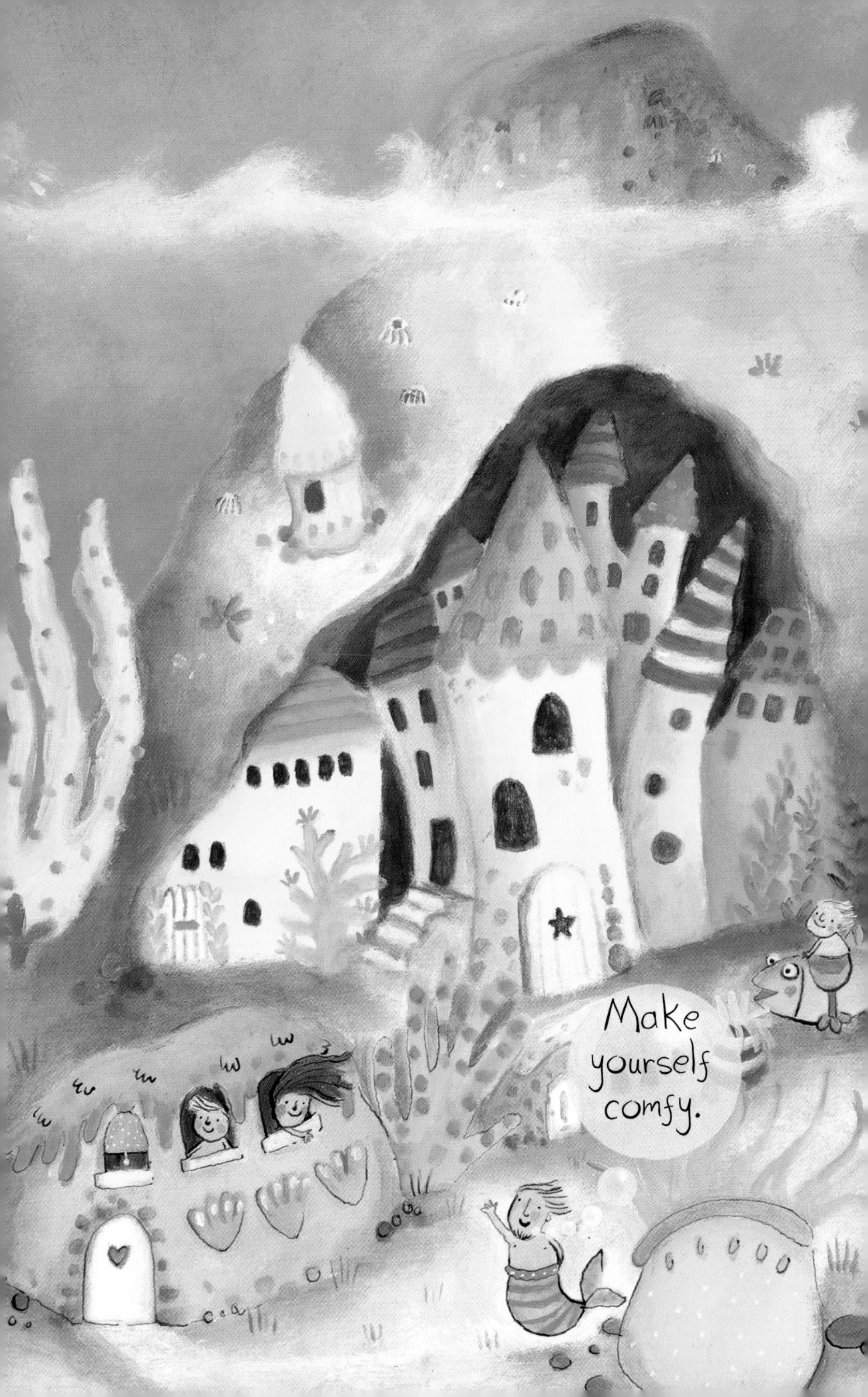
Make yourself comfy.

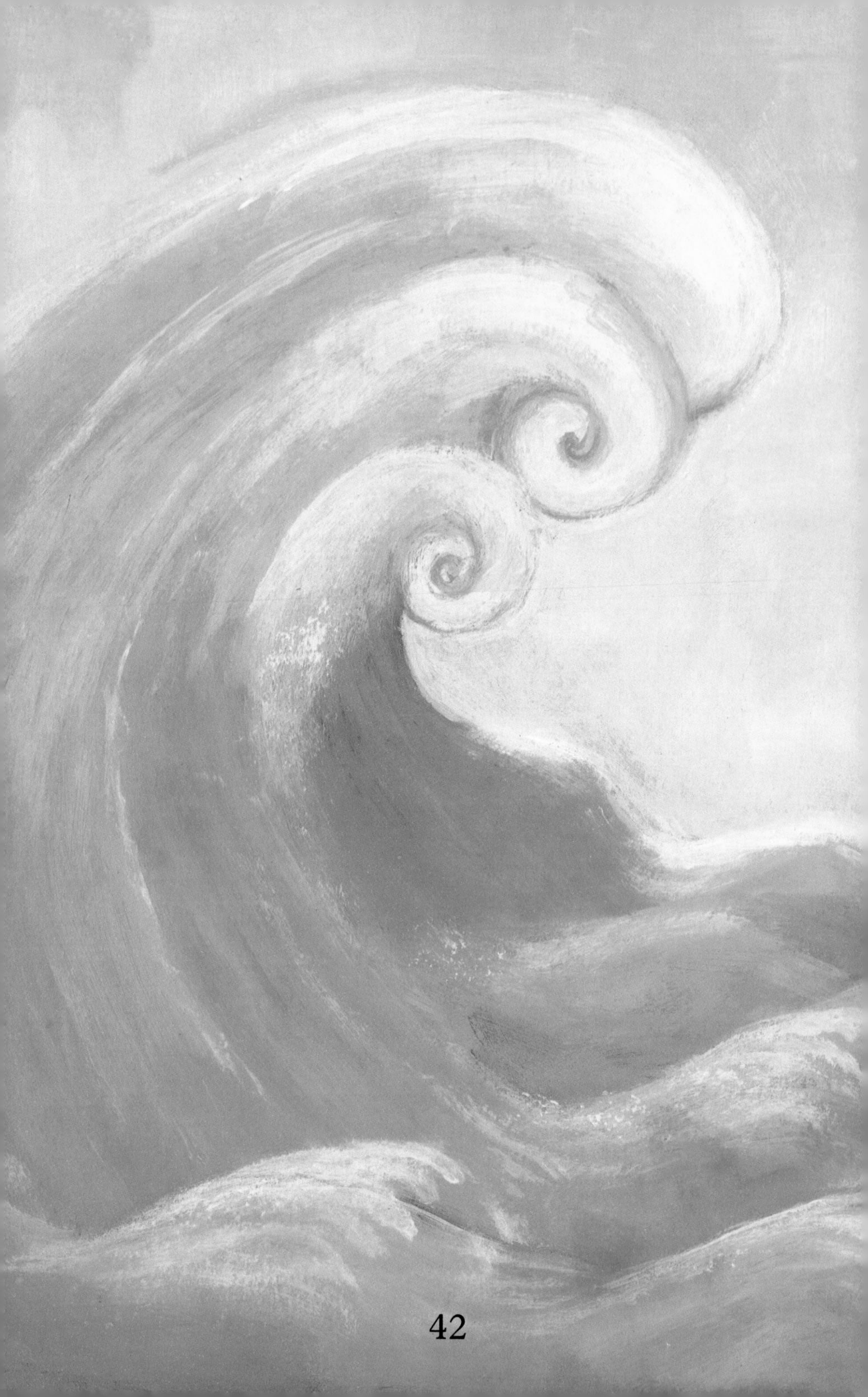

Some time later Robbie was waiting for the next really big wave to come in, waiting for just the right one to dive into. "Look at this one!" he cried as a great green wave came curling in.

It's the biggest yet!

He was just about to dive into it when he
saw what looked like a seal swimming
along the crest of the wave.

But it wasn't a seal, it was Mairi. It was

Mairi swimming!

As she swept past him, his mouth opened in astonishment and the seawater swept in.

"You can swim!" he spluttered.

Mairi's mother and father came running down to the water's edge.

Look at me!

"You can swim!" they cried.

"Of course I can," she said. "It's easy.

I just pretended I was a mermaid."